W9-CNP-223

NOBODY LIVES IN APARTMENT N-2

ANNE SCHRAFF

Artesian Press

P.O. Box 355 Buena Park, CA 90621

Take Ten Books
Mystery

Freeze Frame	1-58659-005-
Cassette	1-58659-010-
The Return of the Eagle	1-58659-002-
Cassette	1-58659-007-
Touchdown	1-58659-003-
Cassette	1-58659-008-
Nobody Lives in Apartment N-2	**1-58659-001-**
Cassette	**1-58659-006-**
Stick Like Glue	1-58659-004-
Cassette	1-58659-009-

Other Take Ten Themes:
Chillers
Sports
Adventure
Disaster
Thrillers
Fantasy

Project Editor: Liz Parker
Cover Illustrator: Marjorie Taylor
Cover Designer: Tony Amaro
Text Illustrator: Fujiko Miller
©2000 Artesian Press

ISBN 1-58659-001-

Chapter 1

"Look," Erick's mom said, "they have the *For Rent* sign up again in that apartment!"

Erick wheeled over to the window. Sure enough—the *For Rent* sign was in the window for about the fifth time this year.

"Something must be wrong over there," Dad looked up from his bacon and eggs long enough to say.

"Maybe the place is haunted," Erick said, half seriously. He loved reading mysteries—even more so since he got stuck in this wheelchair. It had been four years now since the diving accident. The doctors said the spinal cord injury was permanent. Erick figured he might just fool them and walk again someday. But in the meantime, he spent a lot of free time reading mysteries and books about astronomy.

"Probably bad plumbing," Dad said. "Nothing worse than bad plumbing."

Erick and his parents lived on the third floor of the apartment building opposite N-2. Several times as Erick happened to be looking out the window, he saw disturbing things. A red-haired lady came to the window and screamed. Moments later she appeared at the downstairs front door, rushing off with her suitcase. Another time a young couple who lived in N-2 hurried away in the middle of the night as if they were fleeing for their lives. But the worst thing Erick ever saw was what appeared three weeks ago, just before the start of summer vacation.

Erick was up late working on his math final. He wanted to be an astronomer, so he worked extra hard on his math and science classes. After he finished studying, he glanced out the window. There it was in apartment N-2. A pale-faced man with long, matted black hair looking out the window. He looked like he was wearing movie monster make-up. Erick gasped and blinked, and the man was gone. But nobody had rented the apartment since.

Now Erick tried to forget about apartment N-2 and think about his trip to the natural history museum tomorrow with his friend Trung. They were showing a series of pictures of the surface of Mars. Both Erick and Trung were astronomy buffs.

When Trung came in the morning, though, it was apartment N-2 they talked about. "They still can't rent N-2," Erick said.

"That spooky place, eh?" Trung said. Suddenly he grinned. "Have you ever been *in* there, Erick?"

"In apartment N-2? Why no, man!"

Erick said as he wheeled beside Trung down the street.

"We could ask to see it," Trung said. "We could say we're checking it out for some friends."

"Yeah," Erick said. He was eager to see volcanoes on Mars, but the show was running at the museum all summer. Maybe apartment N-2 wouldn't be vacant that long. Erick's skin crawled at the thought of going inside the place, but he was curious, too.

"You're not scared, are you, Erick?" Trung asked. He knew that would do the trick.

"Scared? Me?" Erick laughed. "No way. Let's do it!"

The apartment across the street had elevators like Erick's building so it was no problem getting a wheelchair to the third floor.

"Well, of course you may see the apartment," said Ms. Payson, the apartment manager. She was a tall, slender woman with a needle-thin nose and blue-white hair. The only strange thing about her was that her lower lip trembled sometimes as if she was nervous about something. "Follow me."

The boys followed Ms. Payson onto the elevator. Erick felt a chill go up his spine. He was actually going inside apartment N-2. He muttered silently to himself, "Man, you must be crazy!"

Chapter 2

"It's nice," Erick mumbled, going in first, followed by Trung and Ms. Payson. The carpet was mint green and freshly cleaned. Erick never saw such a clean carpet in his life. The whole apartment smelled like a pine forest, as if someone had madly scrubbed and polished.

"Nice furniture," Trung said, looking around at the plush chairs.

"Yes, it's a fine apartment," Ms. Payson said. Her lower lip trembled.

"What's *that?*" Erick asked, seeing a gaping hole in the living room wall. It looked like someone had taken a sledge hammer to the wall. "Oh ... that. That will be fixed tomorrow. They changed where the television plugs in. The workmen had to break into the wall. That will be . . . uh, fixed," Ms. Payson said. She was nervously rubbing her hands together. She began to pick at her purple nail polish. Erick never saw such ugly nail polish on such short, stubby fingernails.

Trung glanced at a beautiful painting on the living room wall. "That's a great painting," he said. Only it was crooked. When Ms. Payson wasn't looking, he peered behind it. There was another big hole there. The plaster was cracked where the hole had been punched in. It made Trung shudder to think of somebody racing around taking whacks at the walls!

"Well, we'll tell our friends what a nice place this is," Erick said. "Maybe they'll come rent it."

"Yes," Ms. Payson said. She was looking nervously off into the distance as if she expected something horrible to

come down the hall.

"Uh ... I come by here on my way to school," Trung said, "and it seems like this apartment is always for rent. Why do people move away so much?"

"What?" Ms. Payson gasped. Then she tried to smile, but it looked more like a frown. "Oh, there have been problems with the heating ... lots of little things. I'm so ... uh ... tired of it. I've told the owner to just ... ah ... leave it vacant. But he wants to rent it."

When the boys were back down on the street, Erick said, "What do you think, Trung? She was hiding something, don't you think?"

"Yeah, right! And those holes in the walls! There was a big hole behind that painting. Who's going around punching out the walls?" Trung said.

"I saw a movie once," Erick remembered. "Some unearthly force kept smashing stuff in a haunted house."

Trung laughed. "Hey, there's still

time to go see the show at the museum."

"Right," Erick said. He was ready to see the volcanoes on the red planet. But he glanced back one more time at the window of apartment N-2.

"Trung! Look!" Erick shouted.

"What? Where?" Trung asked, his head spinning around.

"Ahhh, he's gone!" Erick said. "I saw that weird pale face with the black hair I told you about. Just now I saw it. He must have been lurking in there when we were looking around!"

"Are you sure?" Trung asked with a sudden grin. "Hey, maybe Ms. Payson puts on monster masks to scare the tenants away, huh?"

"Why would she do that?" Erick asked.

Trung shrugged. "I don't know. It's a funny world, Erick. Who knows why weird people do the stuff they do? I'm telling you, it's scary!"

Chapter 3

Erick and Trung watched the show, amazed at the huge craters on the face of Mars. The speaker said that was proof that huge meteors had struck Mars, causing the craters. There were amazing pictures that also seemed to prove that massive floods once dug channels in Mars. Now only dramatic dust storms changed the environment of the red planet.

After the show, the boys looked at some books in the reception room. "Hey, look here," Erick said, "there's an astronomy camp this summer at Mount Palomar. Wouldn't that be a great place to go? It's in late August, so we could still enroll."

Trung laughed. "What do we use for money for the class? Our good looks?"

"Yeah," Erick said, laughing. "But wouldn't it be super to go? Man, we could look into that great telescope they have. We could hear real astronomers lecture."

"Big stuff for sophomores, huh?" Trung said.

Just then, Ms. Payson appeared behind the boys.

"Oh, hi," Erick said in surprise.

"You must like astronomy, too," Ms. Payson said.

"Yeah, we do," Trung said. "Do you like it, Ms. Payson?"

"Oh, indeed. I love to look at the stars. You can learn a lot from the stars. What is that literature you boys are looking at?"

Erick smiled. "We're California dreaming. There's an astronomy camp for high school students at Mount

Palomar in August. We'd sure like to go."

Trung added, "It costs a lot of money."

"Oh, dear," Ms. Payson said. "Is that a problem?"

"Yeah," Erick said. "Around this neighborhood we're all doing what Dad calls 'keeping one step ahead of the bill collectors.'"

"Well, smart, deserving boys like you should be able to go to such a nice educational camp," Ms. Payson said. She picked up one of the flyers and winked. "Perhaps one of the people in my building would be willing to sponsor you. There are some elderly people there with a bit of money."

"That would be incredible," Trung said.

"We'll see," Ms. Payson said, tucking the flyer in her purse. Then she got the names and addresses of both boys. When she hurried away, the boys looked at each other with the same thought in both of their minds.

"Do you smell something fishy?" Erick asked.

"Yeah," Trung said. "She followed us here and waited for us. It's not just an accident that she ended up here with us."

"Know what I think?" Erick said. "She's afraid we're onto something. She figures we went into apartment N-2 just to nose around. She thinks we suspect there's something rotten going on there. She's scared, Trung."

Trung shook his head. "But we didn't find anything for sure."

"How about those holes in the wall?" Erick said.

"Yeah. Hey, wouldn't it be wild if she got the money for us to go to astronomy camp just to shut us up and make us stop nosing around?" Trung asked.

"That'd be like blackmail, buddy,"

Erick said.

"Yeah," Trung said, shuddering. "Like back in Asia when the government guys made my parents pay blackmail for everything. Bad business."

"There must be something really awful going on in apartment N-2, Trung," Erick said.

Chapter 4

Erick and his parents had moved to this street about a year ago. Trung and his family arrived weeks later, and the boys instantly became friends. They bumped into each other one dawn, while both were trying to spot Venus in the morning sky. Now Erick wondered if the old timers around here might know more about apartment N-2. He decided to ask around.

Erick wheeled down the street the next morning, stopping at the deli on the corner. Benny Hassan had run the deli for five years. He was a friendly guy with a big mustache who always saved special new cheeses for Erick. When Erick mentioned apartment N-2,

Benny nodded.

"The guy in there died about a year ago. Just before you came, Erick. He died on the Fourth of July. I remember all of the noise, then the sirens," Benny said.

"Did you know him?" Erick asked.

"He came in here all of the time. A nice, quiet guy. Always wanted pastrami on rye. It sure was a shock when he died. He fell down in his apartment and busted his head on something. That's what I heard," Benny said.

Farther on down the street Lizzie Hampton, who ran the used clothing store, frowned and said, "I don't believe for a minute that it was an accident. If you ask me, Erick, he was murdered. Hit over the head. That's why they have so much trouble keeping that place rented. Poor fella's ghost is haunting apartment N-2.... If you ask me."

Erick was really excited now. There wasn't just some monkey business going on in apartment N-2. Maybe there had been a murder in there. Lizzie said the dead man's name was Lewis Peters, and he was a loner who'd lived in the apartment for five years. He never worked, but somehow he seemed to get along.

As Erick wheeled past Benny's Deli on the way home, Benny came out. He looked anxious. "Hey, Erick, how come you're so interested in apartment N-2?" he asked.

Erick shrugged. "I don't know. I'm sort of fascinated by mysteries, I guess. I've been seeing weird things in the window over there, and I'd like to know what's going on."

"Well," Benny said, "don't poke around too much. Right after the guy died, I was curious, too. He seemed like a nice little fella, and I couldn't believe he just fell down and died. He was only about forty. I asked too many questions, and one night I got a rock through my window. A note was tied to it. 'Mind your own business. Or else,' the note said. I did. No more curiosity."

"Thanks for the warning, Benny," Erick said. He wheeled the rest of the way home and called Trung right away to give him all of the news.

"Hey, I gotta take my sister to the library, Erick. I'll look in the old newspapers for articles on Lewis Peters. Maybe there will be something there," Trung said.

In the evening, Trung called back. "Hang onto your hat, man," he said. "I found a news story. Turns out Lewis Peters was a big jewel thief! He stole a ton of diamonds from a place in New York. He went to prison, then got out. Is that wild, or what?"

Chapter 5

Trung came over the next day with more from the newspaper article.

"This guy stole over a million bucks in diamonds. He was in the slammer for ten years, but they never found the diamonds, right? Then he gets out, and he rents apartment N-2. Then he dies. So where are the diamonds?" Trung asked.

"That's easy," Erick said. "He stashed them in the walls of apartment N-2. Then, when he died, Ms. Payson, or somebody, starts knocking out holes in the walls looking for them."

"Maybe the guy who owns the apartment building doesn't even know what's going on," Trung said. "And this weird Ms. Payson, she finds ways to scare off the renters so she has an empty apartment to hunt around in."

"Yeah," Erick said. "Maybe she and Peters were friends, and he sort of told her he had the diamonds stashed somewhere in the walls. And then ... Do you think she maybe killed him?"

"That little blue-haired lady?" Trung shook his head. "Man, she looks like a sweet old grandma."

"Was there a picture of that guy Peters in the news article?" Erick asked.

"Yeah. The lady in the library made a copy of the whole article for me." Trung dug the copy from his school bag. He laid it on the table for Erick to look at.

"Hey!" Erick gasped, "That's the guy!"

"What guy?" Trung demanded.

"That's the horrible-looking guy I've seen looking out the window in apartment N-2. Look at that pale, pasty face."

Trung looked more closely. "I saw a prison movie once. The guys in the movie were all pale and ghostly, too. I guess it's because they're locked away so long. But, Erick, you couldn't have seen Peters. He's dead, man! He's been dead for a year!"

"I tell you, it's him," Erick insisted. "Even that matted black hair."

"He's dead!" Trung repeated.

"But I saw him," Erick insisted. "I even remember that big mole on his forehead!"

"Wow, that's really scary," Trung said.

Erick couldn't get apartment N-2 off his mind. He stared out the window every chance he had. He even looked through his telescope sometimes. Apartment N-2 stayed empty, and the frightening face did not appear again over the next week.

At the beginning of the next week,

around dusk, Erick wheeled down to the deli for some cheese. He moved slowly on his way home, watching the lights come on down the dusky street. He loved the flashing neon. Then, as he was almost home, somebody came up behind him, grabbing the back of his wheelchair.

"Kid," said a low raspy voice, "big trucks come rolling down this street sometimes. It would be terrible if your chair sort of slipped under the wheels of one of those big trucks.... Like maybe that cement truck that's coming now ..."

Erick glanced back at the man who had grabbed his chair. He saw a pale, angry face and matted black hair. Erick's blood ran cold.

Chapter 6

The cement truck roared past. Before Erick could yell for help, the man let go of his wheelchair and sprinted away down a dark alley.

Cold sweat poured down Erick's body as he wheeled into his own building and rode up the elevator. He didn't take a full breath until he was behind the double locked doors of his apartment.

Erick called Trung. "I tell you, this awful guy—the one I saw looking out the window of apartment N-2—he came up behind my wheelchair and threatened to push me under a cement truck!"

"Man! Are you sure it was the same

guy?" Trung asked.

"Yeah, I'm sure. Yeah, yeah, I know he's dead and buried and all that, but ..." Erick trailed off.

"A ghost?" Trung asked.

Erick laughed nervously. "Nah, I don't think he's a ghost. Hey, wait. Somebody's at the door."

"Careful, Erick. Don't let anybody in," Trung warned.

"Don't worry, I won't. I'll call you back."

Erick wheeled to the door and peered out the peephole. It was Ms. Payson. Erick wasn't afraid of her, but he thought she was mixed up in something bad. Maybe she had the pale-faced thug with her.

"Hi, Ms. Payson," Erick said through the peephole.

"Oh, Erick, I just came by to bring the good news. An elderly gentleman in the apartment building wants to sponsor you and your friend to go to that astronomy camp. Are your parents home?"

"Wow, that sounds great. My folks will be home around six," Erick said.

"Fine. I'll be by at seven," she said.

Erick told his parents about the offer when they got home.

"What's the deal?" Dad asked. "You don't get anything for nothing."

"It doesn't sound right to me that a perfect stranger wants to sponsor you two boys," Mom said.

"Well," Erick admitted, "I've been nosing around apartment N-2, and I think Ms. Payson would rather I didn't."

"You mean the money would be to stop you from poking your nose into funny business over there, eh?" Dad asked.

"Maybe," Erick said.

Ms. Payson came at 7:00 as she'd promised. She seemed very nervous. Her chin trembled, and her purple fingernail polish was almost picked completely off. Her hands shook as she pulled the check from her purse. "This elderly gentleman ... ah ... believes in supporting the dreams of the next generation," she explained.

"Ms. Payson," Erick said, "is somebody upset about me and my friend looking around apartment N-2?"

Ms. Payson turned pale. She almost dropped the check. "Why ... I ... uh, don't know what you're talking about!"

Erick thought about the thug who had threatened him and now the old man who offered to send him to camp. Both wanted Erick to do the same thing—forget about what was happening in apartment N-2.

Ms. Payson dabbed at her eyes for a moment. Then she said, "All right. There have been unfortunate problems in the building. The man died mysteriously . . . and other things. Never mind. We just don't want anybody stirring up old bones." She looked at Erick's parents. "I see nothing wrong in … well … if the boys will just stay out of things that do not concern them, we would be … ah … grateful." She waved the check in the air.

"I don't want it," Erick said. "It'd be like selling my soul."

Chapter 7

"I respect what you did, Erick," Dad said when Ms. Payson left. "But we don't want you messing around with this evil business anymore. Let the police figure out what's happening over in apartment N-2."

"That's right," Mom said. "It's downright scary to get involved in something like that."

"Okay," Erick agreed. "No more going over there." But that didn't mean Erick didn't intend to keep an eye out that window sometimes. After all, he could always say he was searching the sky for stars!

Trung did some more checking in the library, too. He found out that Mr.

Peters had a sad little funeral. Only his brother from out of town came.

"His brother, eh?" Erick wondered aloud. An idea came to him. Maybe they were *twin* brothers, identical twins. Maybe Lewis Peters had a brother who looked just like him, with a pale face and matted black hair. Now the brother was hanging around, searching for the diamonds and trying to scare people away.

Erick had a friend down at the police station. Sergeant Janet Tremayne had helped everybody form a neighborhood watch program about six months ago, and she even visited the schools. Erick figured she'd be nice enough to tell him a few basics about the Lewis Peters case.

"What? Do you want to be a detective, Erick?" she asked, laughing.

"Yeah, I want to solve the mysteries of the universe. I want to be an astronomer. But I'm curious about this apartment across the street where a Lewis Peters died. Some people in the neighborhood say he was murdered, and some say it was an accident. So what was it?" Erick asked.

"Well, the case is still open. It looked like an accident, but there were unanswered questions," Sgt. Tremayne said.

"I was wondering about the guy's brother. He wasn't a twin or anything, was he?" Erick asked.

Sgt. Tremayne laughed again. "Where did you get that idea? Oscar Peters was a little bald guy who seemed afraid of his shadow. Drab. Colorless. Worked as a make-up man in a wax museum in Philadelphia! He just came, buried his brother, and left town."

Erick thanked the sergeant and wheeled for home. Another good idea gone sour. No twin brother, just a poor little character who did his duty in burying his bad brother and leaving town!

In the afternoon Erick and Trung had cheeseburgers at the neighborhood diner.

"Maybe the whole thing is just a lot of spooky nothing," Trung said.

"That ugly guy who tried to push me under a cement truck was real," Erick said.

"Yeah," Trung said, nibbling on a french fry. "You're right."

"And the guy in the window—the same guy who threatened me—he's real, Trung. I swear he was there!" Erick said.

"Do you believe in ghosts?" Trung finally asked.

"I don't know," Erick said. "I'm not sure."

"Me neither. There could be ghosts. Maybe what we have here is . . . well

. . . the ghost of old Peters!" Trung said.

As the boys headed home, Erick glanced up at apartment N-2. A pretty girl was looking out the window. She was smiling. Someone in N-2! Erick shuddered at the thought of it.

Chapter 8

Erick met the new tenant down at Benny's Deli the next day. He recognized the same pretty girl with the long, dark hair. She was talking to Benny.

"We're new in the neighborhood. Just me and Mom. I'm a computer operator, and Mom does sewing. If you hear of anybody who needs sewing, here's her business card."

"I'll keep it handy," Benny promised.

When the girl left, Erick told Benny she was living in apartment N-2. Benny whistled.

Nothing happened for a week. Erick saw the girl going to work every day.

Then, one night as Erick was trying to spot some stars in the sky, his telescope caught the dark-haired girl at the window. She had thrown the window open and was waving her hands as if to drive smoke out. But there was no smoke. Finally she disappeared.

Erick met the girl at the deli the next morning.

"Hi," Erick said. "I live opposite you in the apartment across the street. I was worried about you last night. You seemed to be trying to sweep smoke out the window."

"Oh, did we ever make a mistake moving in there! The smell is terrible," the girl said.

"Oh, yeah?" Erick asked.

"It smelled okay when we moved in. But now there's a really awful odor and thumping on the walls. Mom is in bed with a sick headache all the time," the girl said.

Erick said, "Nobody lives long in

apartment N-2. It's always for rent."

"I'm not surprised. We're moving as soon as we can—maybe even tomorrow. Ms. Payson is being nice about it. She's going to give us back the rent and the deposit and everything. She's even helping us move."

"Did Ms. Payson say what was causing the bad smell?" Erick asked.

"She said something about cats in the basement. But this doesn't smell like cats. And the thumping!" The girl held herself and shook.

Erick told her about Mr. Peters dying in apartment N-2.

"Oh, wow!" the girl said, her eyes getting big. "Maybe the place is haunted, huh? Oh, boy, I'd better not tell Mom about the dead guy until we're outta there."

The girl hurried from the deli, and Erick thought maybe he'd said too much. But it was too late to worry about that now. He wheeled home and watched a television special on astronomy.

At around 4:00 the next afternoon, Ms. Payson phoned Erick's apartment.

"Hello, Erick," she said in a nervous little voice. "I have no one to talk to about this except you. I know that you have seen enough of the horrible things going on to understand and not laugh at me."

"What's up, Ms. Payson?" Erick asked.

"It's just that I can't stand this anymore. I'm not a young woman. This job is impossible. The owners expect me to keep the place rented, but I cannot! I am sick to death of the horror of apartment N-2! I must tell you the truth. *Someone must know the truth!*"

"What is the truth, Ms. Payson?" Erick asked.

"He's here. *He's always been here!* Bothering me. Bothering the people who move into apartment N-2," she said. She seemed near tears.

"Who's there, Ms. Payson!" Erick asked.

"That devil—that thief—Lewis Peters, of course!" Ms. Payson gasped.

Chapter 9

"But he's dead," Erick pointed out. "Lewis Peters died, didn't he?"

Ms. Payson was sobbing wildly now over the phone. "No, no. He's upstairs right now, gathering his diamonds. He has an ax, and he's breaking into the walls! Oh, I know he died and all that, but it hasn't stopped him—or his ghost!"

"You'd better call the police, Ms. Payson," Erick said.

"The police! They would laugh at me. They would call me a crazy old lady. You must be my witness. You've seen him at the window, haven't you? Haven't you?"

"Well, yeah, I've seen this pale

guy," Erick answered, wondering how Ms. Payson knew that.

"That's him!" she cried. "I'm leaving now, Erick. I'm packing my things and going. When the owner of the building comes and wants to know why apartment N-2 is smashed up, you tell him, Erick. Tell him I stood it as long as I could, as long as anybody could. Tell him Lewis Peters did it. He smashed everything and drove me away." She hung up quickly.

Erick stared from the window. Sure enough, Ms. Payson soon appeared downstairs, dragging a heavy suitcase on wheels out the front door. She climbed into her old Chevrolet and backed up to the door. She loaded the suitcase with difficulty. Erick figured it contained all of her important possessions.

Running, she went to the door on the driver's side, almost stumbled getting in, and then drove off. Erick wrote down her license plate number. He didn't know exactly why he did that, but something told him to.

Erick looked up at the window. He expected to see the frightening face with the matted hair peering out. After all, the ghost had won, hadn't it? It had driven everybody out, even Ms. Payson. But there was just emptiness at the window.

Erick called Trung. He told him what had happened.

"I guess we'd better call the police," Trung said.

"Yeah," Erick agreed.

Sgt. Tremayne and two other officers came over. They inspected the apartment. Just as Ms. Payson had said, it was smashed up. The walls had all been broken into with an ax.

"Looks like the work of a madman, all right," one of the detectives said.

"She said it was the ghost of Lewis

Peters. He was looking for the diamonds that he hid when he was alive," Erick said. "But I don't think it was a ghost who did this." Erick took the license plate number from his pocket and handed it to Sgt. Tremayne. "I bet Ms. Payson is heading for the airport. She's driving a beat-up Chevy. Here's the license plate number," he said.

Sgt. Tremayne smiled. "Thank you, Erick," she said.

Chapter 10

They brought Ms. Payson back to the apartment building in less than an hour. Just as Erick figured, she was heading for the airport with a one-way ticket to Philadelphia.

Erick, Trung, and a lot of other neighbors were waiting on the sidewalk as Ms. Payson returned in a police car. They watched as Ms. Payson got out of the police car, with an officer holding her arm tightly.

"I don't understand this at all," she said in a cold voice. She spotted Erick and said, "Didn't you tell them what happened? Didn't you tell them all that I'd been through? Didn't you explain about the ghost?"

One of the detectives peered into the bulging suitcase and shouted, "Bingo! Bags of uncut diamonds. There must be a fortune here."

Erick figured that was what had made him suspicious, watching Ms. Payson struggling with that heavy bag. He thought it must have had more inside than dresses.

"Nosy little punks," Ms. Payson screamed, seeing that she was caught. "It's all your fault!" She looked bitterly at Erick and Trung.

Then, slowly, the voice changed as her act ended. The woman's high-pitched voice became a man's harsh voice. The blue-white wig went crooked and fell to the street, revealing a shiny bald head.

One of the detectives found a mask in the car. It was the carefully made mask of a pale-faced man with matted black hair and a mole on the forehead. It was a mask made to look just like

Lewis Peters!

"You're Oscar Peters," Sgt. Tremayne said.

It turned out that Oscar had come to his brother's apartment that night in July. They argued about money. Oscar demanded some of the diamonds. A fight followed. Lewis Peters fell from a blow. He struck his head on a glass table and died.

Oscar knew the stolen diamonds had to be in apartment N-2. He didn't have enough money to rent the place himself. So he put on make-up and a wig to look like an old lady. He got hired as apartment manager because he offered to work so cheap.

Oscar made the mask of his brother easily. After all, he worked at a wax museum. He used the mask and other tricks to scare people from N-2 so he had a vacant place to search. Breaking into the walls, he found dozens of small sacks of uncut diamonds. He finally found the last sack last night.

"Hey, Trung," Erick said on Friday, "guess what? There's a reward for the return of those stolen diamonds."

"No kidding?" Trung said.

Erick laughed and said, "Guess who's going to Mount Palomar to the Astronomy camp after all—you and me, buddy!"

The boys did a high five and shouted so loudly that even a ghost in apartment N-2 would have been frightened away.